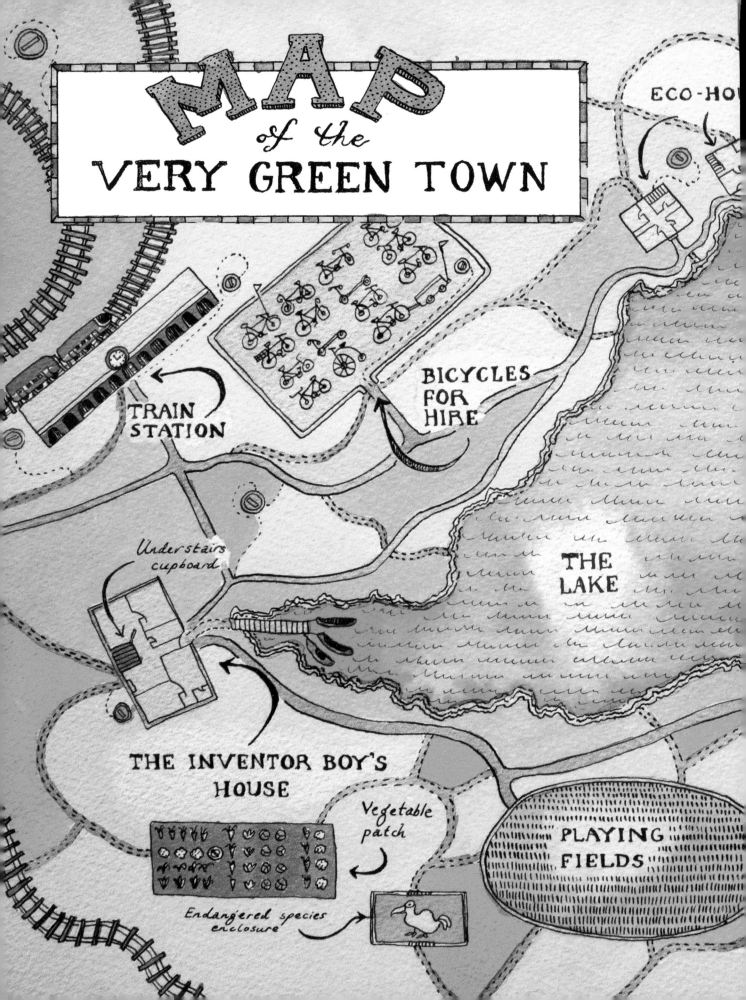

THE ISLAND

Recycling Plant

The apple tree

Jetty

FOREST

Greenhouses

SCHOOL

2.

4. 7.

8.

6.

5.

Archery targets

3. 9. 1. 10.

N
NW NE
W E
SW SE
S

1. Language Laboratory. 2. Gargoyle cage. 3. Acrobatics hall. 4. Maths cell.
5. History tower. 6. Virtual Reality programming pod. 7. Music room.
8. Geography bunker 9. Chemistry laboratory. 10. Telescope workshop.

Published by:
World Future Council Foundation
Mexikoring 29
22297 Hamburg
Germany
www.worldfuturecouncil.org

and

Disbributed by:
Voices of Future Generations Series of Children's Books
Chancellor Day Hall 3644 Peel Street Montreal, Quebec H3A 1W9
www.voicesoffuturegenerations.org

Special thanks to René V. Steiner for excellent layout and graphics:
www.steinergraphics.com.
Highest thanks also to CPI Books, for outstanding printing and delivery
services, as part of CPI's corporate social responsibility contribution:
www.cpibooks.com/uk.

The 'Voices of Future Generations' Series
'The Inventor Boy and His Little Brother' (Book 1)

 UN Committee on the Rights of the Child

This book is printed on recycled paper, using sustainable and low-carbon printing methods.   ISBN 978-3-00-047937-3

the
epic
eco-inventions

by

jona
david

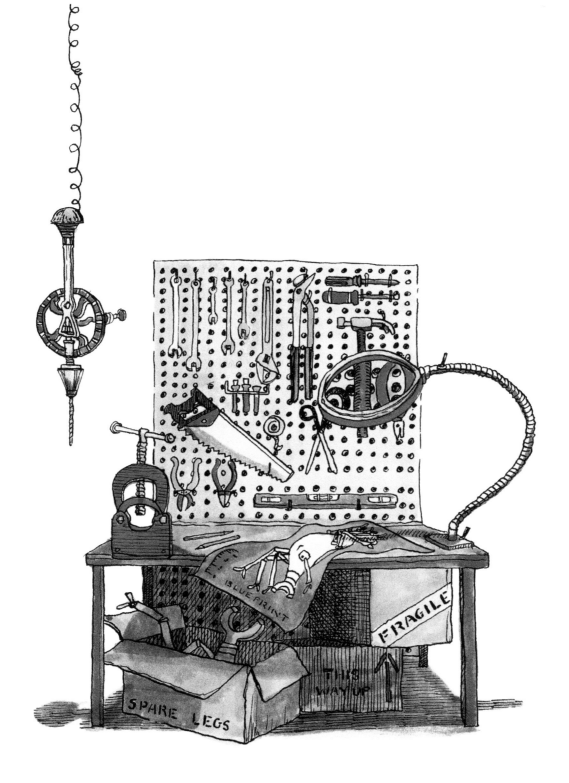

foreword

It gives me much pleasure to contribute this preface to a volume which is the first of a series of children's books: *Voices of Future Generations.*

This volume demonstrates how deeply children contemplate international peace and justice, sustainable development and human rights on which the future of civilisation depends. In a time of climate change, denigration of resources, environmental pollution and other challenges, this series will convey, in a charming way, the message of the younger generation to us, indicating their concern to help in the creation of the better world of the future. They stress also the importance of the sacred trust that our generation carries, to help in constructing a better world for them.

This imaginative little story is a call to all of us. It is a reminder of the importance of hope, courage, creativity, kindness and environmental responsibility—key qualities for our civilisations to flourish in the future. The child author, whom I have known nearly all of his life, has a bright and curious mind, a true heart, a courageous spirit and an intense commitment to protecting the earth and its peoples in peace. By helping his voice to be heard, we offer hope.

As lawyer and judge, and even more importantly as father and grandfather, I have had many occasions to contemplate the future world order of which our children will be a part. This book offers many perspectives on this all-important question. I warmly commend it and the series of which it forms a part.

— *HE Judge C.G. Weeramantry*
UNESCO Peace Education Prize Laureate,
Former Vice-President, International Court of Justice & Patron,
Centre for International Sustainable Development Law (CISDL),
Councillor of the World Future Council

At the World Future Council, we are dedicated to our responsibility to pass on a healthy planet to our children and grandchildren. By representing a strong voice and speaking out on behalf of future generations, we are working hard to close the gap between what we should be doing, and what is already being done right now. This remarkable book series provides a voice to you, young people. Through these new stories, we share two key promises that the world has made to our future generations: the *Convention on the Rights of the Child* and *The Future We Want* Declaration.

— *Jakob von Uexküll,*
Founder and Chair, Management Board, World Future Council and
Founder of the Right Livelihood Award

prefaces

Sustainable development has been the overarching goal of the international community since the 1992 Earth Summit of the United Nations. We know that using the limited resources provided by our Earth in a way that will leave little to future generations is an infringement of their human rights. Inter-generational equity is especially critical when children—the future generations—and their rights are involved.

Science plays a key role in a more sustainable world. In this book, a little boy and his brother illustrate how science, when used in a just and honest way, could change the world for the better.

The children's book series *Voices of Future Generations* provides the ideal platform for linking the issues of children's rights and sustainable development as well as giving young authors the opportunity to show us adults how they envisage the future. Dear young authors and readers—I look forward to learning from you.

— Dr Julia Marton-Lefèvre
Director General of the International Union for Conservation of Nature (IUCN) &
Councillor of the World Future Council

On the occasion of the 25th Anniversary of the UN Convention on the Rights of the Child, I would like to stress the importance of listening to the voices of children. The global challenges we face today, including conflict, epidemics and climate change, have particularly serious consequences for children and are of crucial concern to them. We need to involve children in our search for solutions to these challenges. All children should be invited to participate in this work. The new book series 'Voices of Future Generations' aims to help realise the rights of children to participate and be heard in decisions which affect them. Jona's voice is imaginative, joyful and true, representing children's fears and hopes for future generations, and the Committee on the Rights of the Child fully endorses his call for environmental education programmes. I commend the series for its dedication to share children's voices with readers globally. With their creativity, commitment and hopeful visions, the child authors can inspire us all to find the necessary will and resources to cooperate for sustainable solutions.

—Professor Kristen Sandberg
University of Oslo, Chairperson of the UN Committee on the Rights of the Child

The United Nations Convention on the Rights of the Child

All children are holders of important human rights. Twenty-five years ago in 1989, over a hundred countries agreed a UN Convention on the Rights of the Child. In the most important human rights treaty in history, they promised to protect and promote all children's equal rights, which are connected and equally important.

In the 54 Articles of the Convention, countries make solemn promises to defend children's needs and dreams. They recognize the role of children in realizing their rights, being heard and involved in decisions. Especially, Article 24 and Article 27 defend children's rights to safe drinking water, good food, a clean and safe environment, health, quality of life. And Article 29 recognizes children's rights to education that develops personality, talents and potential, respecting human rights and the natural environment.

— *Alexandra Wandel, Samia Kassid*
World Future Council

The United Nations Declaration on the Future We Want

At the United Nations Rio+20 Conference on Sustainable Development in 2012, governments and people came together to find pathways for a safer, more fair, and greener world for all. Everyone agreed to take new action to end poverty, stop environmental problems, and build bridges to a more just future. In 283 paragraphs of *The Future We Want* Declaration, countries committed to defend human rights, steward resources, fight climate change and pollution, protect animals, plants and biodiversity, and look after oceans, mountains, wetlands and other special places.

It inspired new sustainable development goals for the whole world, with targets for real actions on the ground. Clubs, governments, firms, schools and people like you started 700+ partnerships, and mobilized over $515 billion. The future we want exists in the hearts and minds of our leaders, and in the hands of us all.

— *Vuyelwa Kuuya, Carissa Wong*
Centre for International Sustainable Development Law (CISDL)

chapter 1

In a house by a lake in a very green town there lived a boy and his little brother.

Secretly, the boy was a Mad Genius Inventor.

But no one knew this—not even his little brother, at first. The boy told no-one about his inventions. He did not want them to be scared or to laugh at him.

His parents would sometimes tell him off when he came home with strange stains and tears in his clothes.

Once, they even found a large piece of Delphiniorite (an element he had just discovered) in his sports bag.

The boy and his little brother went to what the neighbours called 'A Terribly Good School'.

They studied:

maths,
astro-physics,
acrobatics,
chemistry and biology,
care of endangered species,
virtual reality programming,
telescope repair,
geography,
archery,
music,

AND

gargoyle maintenance.

They also studied lots and lots of languages.

The boy's little brother was joyful. He loved music and spoke many languages.

For birthdays and other celebrations he received many toys from his brother.

At first, the little brother did not realise that they were special. He thought his big brother had found his presents in the toyshops!

He got ...

1. A pet robot spider that 'turns invisible'.

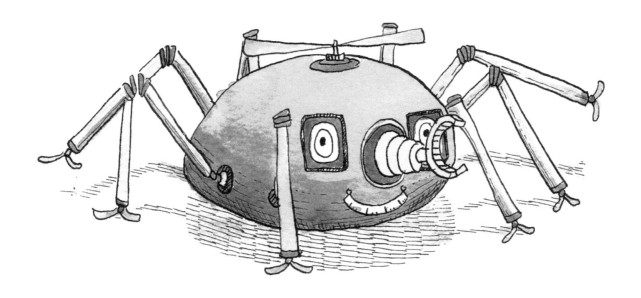

1. BLUEPRINT NOTES: PET ROBOT SPIDER

1. Force-field to bend light for invisibility effect
2. Positronic brain
3. Tiny nebula-fuel gas cells
4. Special steel and crazy glue web spinner

CONFIDENTIAL

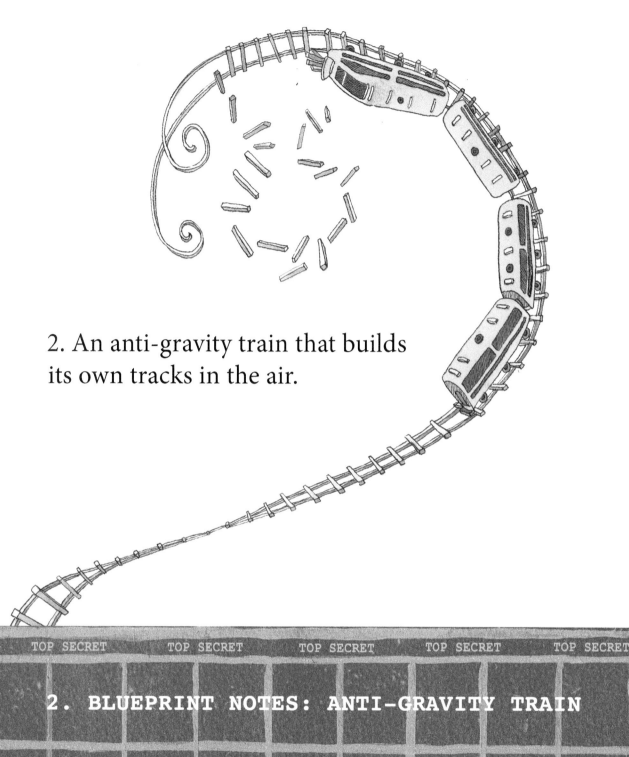

2. An anti-gravity train that builds its own tracks in the air.

2. BLUEPRINT NOTES: ANTI-GRAVITY TRAIN

1. Super light hyper-plastic
2. Nanotech rods that rebuild and fold track
3. Remote control pointer for directing train
4. Nebula gas fuel cells

EYES ONLY

17

3. An ultra-light eco-spaceship that paints words on the ceiling.

3. BLUEPRINT NOTES: ECO-SPACESHIP

1. Spray paint (evaporating ink)
2. Super-cooled ink tank (non-evaporating)
3. Positronic robot brain with language components
4. Nebula gas fuel cells

CONFIDENTIAL

4. A light-maze that makes organic sweets.

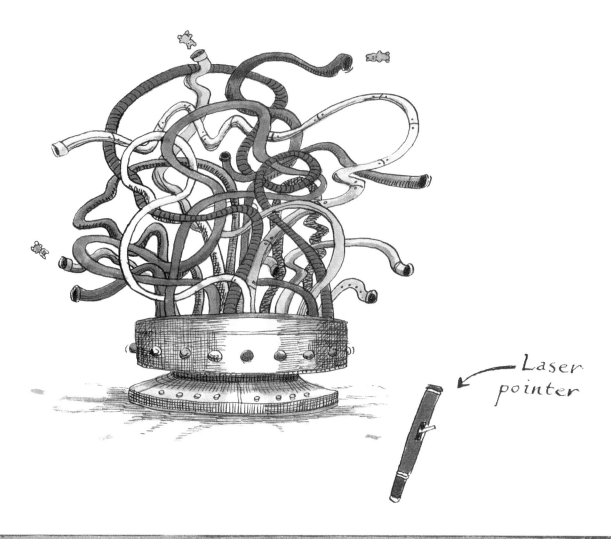

Laser pointer

4. BLUEPRINT NOTES: LIGHT MAZE

1. Transparent glass for laser-guiding tubes
2. Circular base and sweet maker
3. Delphiniorite and hyper-plastic for positronic scrambler unit
4. Nebula gas, metal, and delphiniorite glass

And at school, the children loved the little brother's stories.

Everyone thought they just came from his imagination.

Everyone—apart from the school bully.

chapter 2

On their first day after Christmas break, the boys had their maths, science, and English lessons.

The little brother's pet robot spider had followed him to school—but he didn't realise, because it was invisible.

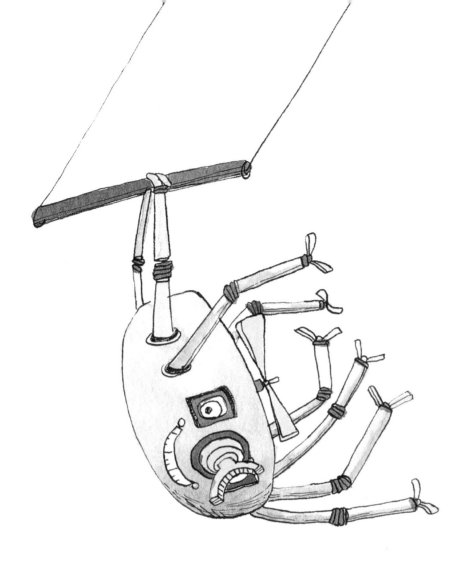

The spider robot went to all his classes.

It particularly liked gymnastics.

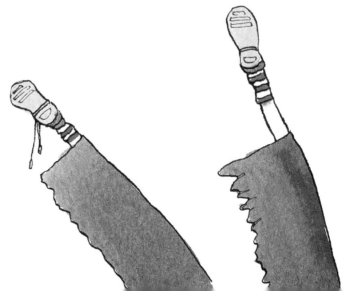

On their way home the spider appeared and did some tricks.

But when the school bully saw it, he threatened them and the robot spider.

The little ones were scared, but they tried to be brave. They called for help.

Luckily, the Mad Genius Inventor Boy saw that his little brother was in trouble. Quickly, he activated the forcefield watch that he'd just invented.

It spun out, acting as a shield, driving the bully away.

Their friends were amazed!

For the first time, the little brother started to see that maybe his toys were rather ... unusual.

Afterwards, the boys invited their brave friends home for a picnic.

They took their canoe out to the island in the middle of the lake.

They had a great time there, playing hide-and-seek with the pet robot spider.

While they played, the little brother noticed
a lever on the side of the island's apple tree.

'I'll come back soon and
investigate', he thought.

chapter 3

The Inventor Boy had a habit of disappearing for hours at a time, especially in the early mornings when everyone else was asleep.

The little brother decided to investigate the lever in the tree.

So one afternoon after school he and his pet robot spider snuck away.

When he got to the tree, he pulled
the lever.

A secret door opened up, with a
marvellous glass elevator
leading underground.

As the little brother went deep into the Earth, a huge laboratory became visible.

It was full of physics, chemistry and biology equipment, as well as many half-built inventions.

There were...

1. Personal jet-packs with 'solar propellors'.

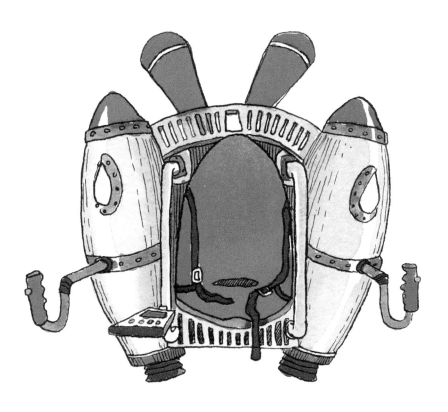

1. BLUEPRINT NOTES: JET PACKS

1. Solar propellors for recharging while flying ...
2. Control belt for direction ...
3. Special sun-protection goggles with infra-red for night flying ...
4. Hydro-dynamic 'underwater' mode, with retractable scuba gear.

CONFIDENTIAL

2. A lightning re-charger that can charge non-electrical things.

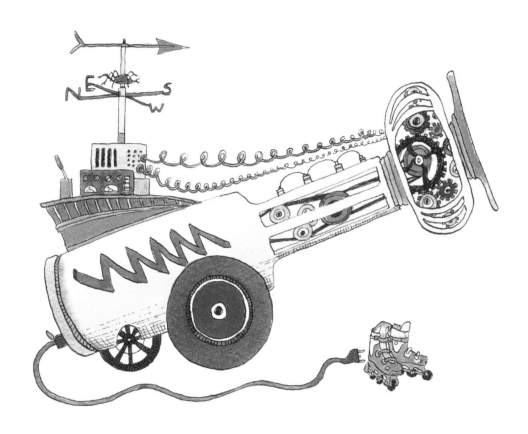

2. BLUEPRINT NOTES: LIGHTNING RE-CHARGER

1. Lightning meltdown protector shells …
2. Calibrator energy field matcher to avoid circuit burnout …
3. Weathervane lightning attractor …
4. Lightning storage cells.

3. A magma drill that uses geothermal power for construction 'projects'.

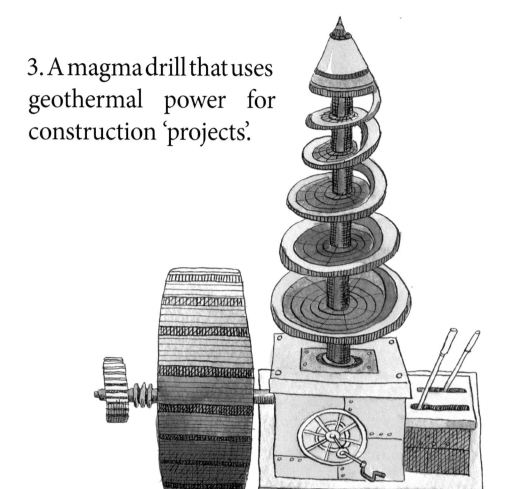

3. BLUEPRINT NOTES: GEOTHERMAL MAGMA DRILL

1. Delphiniorite and diamond super-hard mobile drill-head
2. Hyper-sonic boosters to soften materials prior to drilling
3. Magma heat treatment to soften rock
4. Geothermal super-conductor roots for power source

CONFIDENTIAL

4. A zoo of mechanical animals that can build their own 'nano-habitats'.

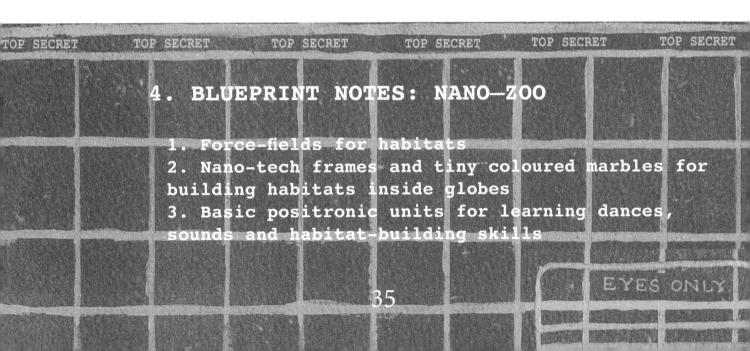

4. BLUEPRINT NOTES: NANO—ZOO

1. Force-fields for habitats
2. Nano-tech frames and tiny coloured marbles for building habitats inside globes
3. Basic positronic units for learning dances, sounds and habitat-building skills

There was even a special nebula gas fuel cell invention.

The fuel cell machine, which looked like a large computer with a satellite dish, could directly harness energy from the universe and store it in renewable energy cells, with clouds of swirling purple light.

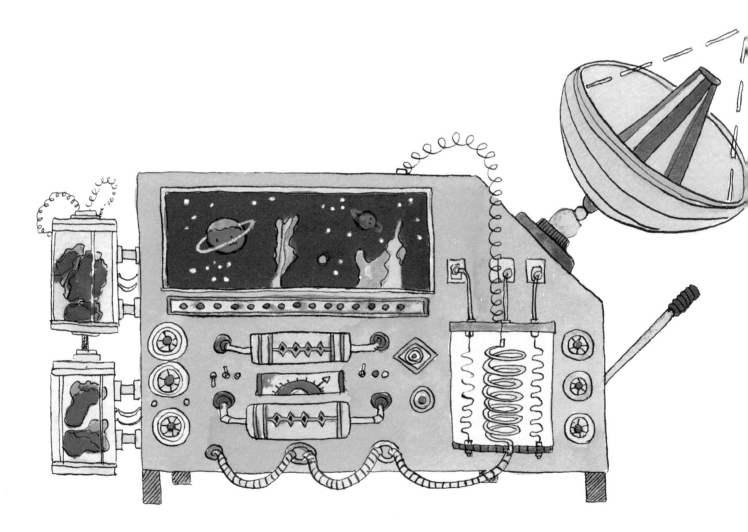

Suddenly, everything made sense! The brilliant toys ... his brother's disappearances ... their home's never-ending power supply. ... and the special dashboard on their family hybrid car that read 'flight mode!'

The little boy was astonished. He realised his brother was a Mad Genius Inventor!

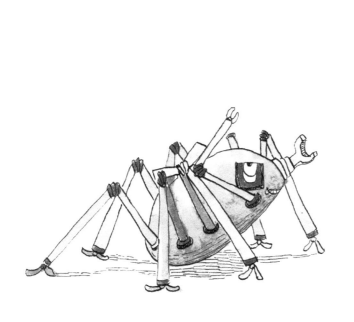

In one corner of the underground lab there was a strange trampoline platform. When the little brother and his pet robot spider climbed up on it, the bounce made them float. It was a disguised anti-gravity machine!

The more they explored, the more they saw.

One wall had a giant control panel, with screens and millions of buttons saying things like 'activate force field'.

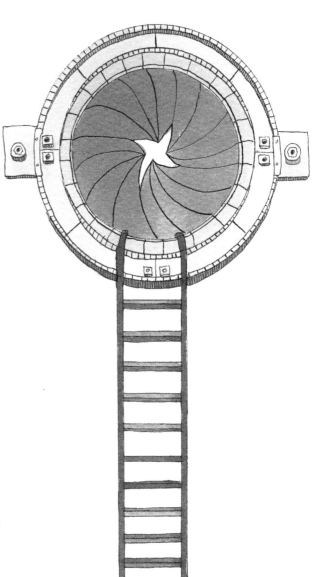

Suddenly, the spider activated its chirp alarm.

They heard footsteps — someone was coming!

chapter 4

The hatch opened, and the Mad Genius Inventor Boy appeared. When he saw his little brother, he laughed.

'I guess I couldn't keep all this secret forever'. he said.

Then the Inventor Boy showed them the tunnel he had come from.

It was long, and dark ...

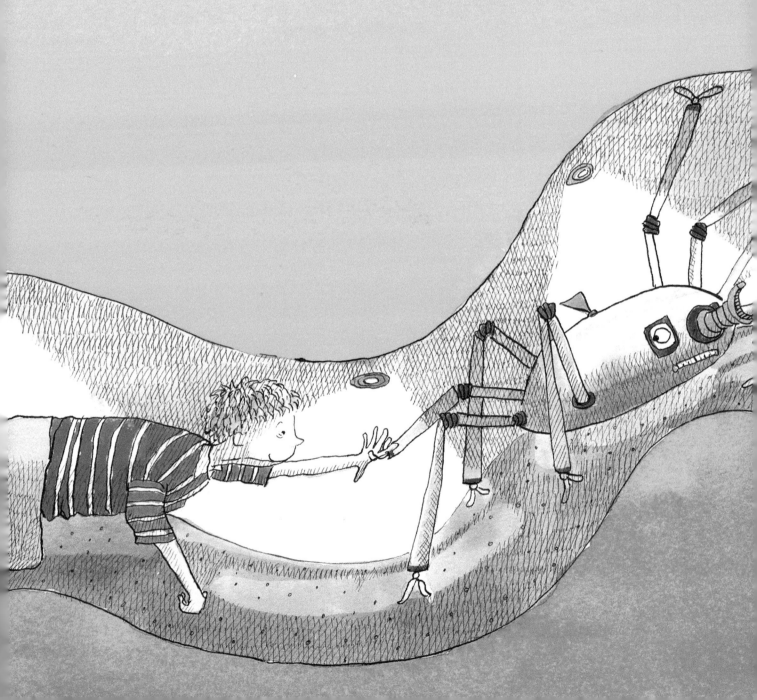

leading right underneath the lake!

The tunnel came up under their own home,
in the cupboard under the stairs!

But while the boys were exploring, an awful
thing happened.

The school bully had taken a horribly loud motor boat out on the lake.

When he saw the little brother's canoe, he stopped at the island.

He looked around for a while, and then he saw a secret hatch in the grass.

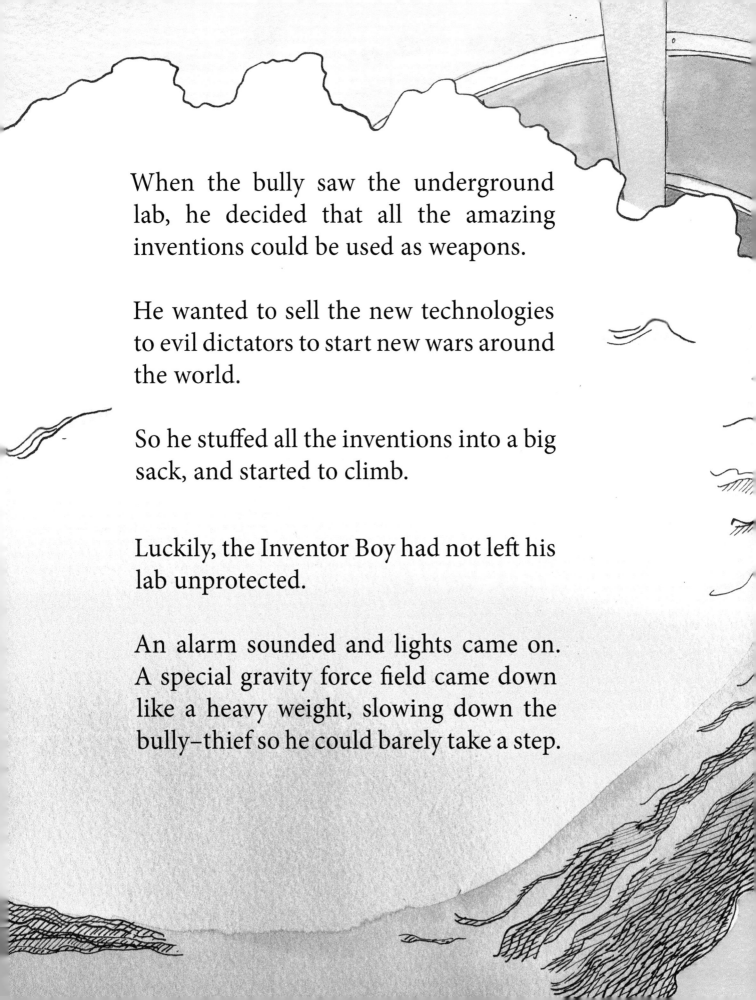

When the bully saw the underground lab, he decided that all the amazing inventions could be used as weapons.

He wanted to sell the new technologies to evil dictators to start new wars around the world.

So he stuffed all the inventions into a big sack, and started to climb.

Luckily, the Inventor Boy had not left his lab unprotected.

An alarm sounded and lights came on. A special gravity force field came down like a heavy weight, slowing down the bully–thief so he could barely take a step.

Just as the bully struggled to the top of the ladder, the little brother's pet robot spider darted forward.

He threw out his web, like a bolt of silver lightning, tangling up the bully–thief. The bully fell to the ground, totally trapped.

Soon the Inventor Boy and his little brother arrived, alerted by the alarm. They took the bully–thief straight to the police. He was given two conducts, and agreed to do community service so he could learn to be a better person.

chapter 5

The Mad Genius Inventor Boy, his little brother and their happy pet robot spider headed home in their canoe. They decided it was time to tell everyone about the inventions.

The little brother was worried that if they did not share them, others might steal them and use them for evil. 'It's worth being laughed at if your inventions can help clean up the Earth and end poverty', he said.

When they shared them, everyone was amazed. Their parents even ran out and got them licences for everything to protect the boy's work.

Then the little brother packed the renewable energy machine, the anti-gravity trampoline, the invisibity gadget, and many other eco-toys for children into a large, sturdy suitcase.

During the holidays, the little brother travelled the world, using his knowledge of many languages to share the Inventor Boy's technologies with leaders of countries who wanted peace and a clean environment.

Many schools were working to start new environmental education programmes, as a clean environment is one of children's human rights.

They were very pleased to see him and the inventions, because he was so joyful, and the inventions were so clever and useful for learning about eco-science and technology.

Meanwhile the Inventor Boy was hard at work in his lab on his next ideas, and people all over the planet were using his new green inventions to learn and live better.

And the inventor boy always asked his little brother when he got home—what did you see?

And the little brother always answered, 'Oh ... the future. The future we want.'

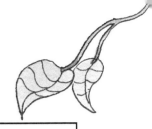

Thanks and Inspiring Resources

'Voices of Future Generations' International Commission
Warmest thanks to the International Commission, chaired by His Excellency Judge CG Weeramantry, which supports, guides and profiles this new series of Children's Books Series, including Ms Alexandra Wandel (WFC), Dr Marie-Claire Cordonier Segger (CISDL), Dr Kristiann Allen (New Zealand), Ms Irina Bokova (UNESCO), Mr Karl Hansen (Trust for Sustainable Living), Dr Maria Leichner-Reynal (Uruguay), Ms Melinda Manuel (PNG), Ms Julia Marton-Lefevre (IUCN), Dr James Moody (Australia), Ms Anna Oposa (The Philippines), Ms Belinda Rasmussen (UK), Professor Kirsten Sandberg (UN CRC Chair), Mr Nikhil Seth / Ms Patricia Chaves (UN DSD), Dr Marcel Szabo (Hungary), Dr Christina Voigt (Norway), Ms Adriana Zacarias (Mexico) and others.

The World Future Council consists of 50 eminent global changemakers from across the globe. Together, they work to pass on a healthy planet and just societies to our children and grandchildren. (www.worldfuturecouncil.org)

United Nations Education, Science and Culture Organization (UNESCO) which celebrates its 70th Anniversary throughout 2015, strives to build networks among nations that enable humanity's moral and intellectual solidarity by mobilizing for education, building intercultural understanding, pursuing scientific cooperation, and protecting freedom of expression. (en.unesco.org)

The **United Nations Committee on the Rights of the Child (CRC)** is the body of 18 independent experts that monitors implementation of the Convention on the Rights of the Child, and its three Optional Protocols, by its State parties. (www.ohchr.org)

United Nations Environment Programme (UNEP) provides leadership and encourages partnership in caring for the environment by inspiring, informing, and enabling nations and peoples to improve their quality of life without compromising that of future generations. (www.unep.org)

International Union for the Conservation of Nature (IUCN) envisions a just world that values and conserves nature, working to conserve the integrity and diversity of nature and to ensure that any use of natural resources is equitable and ecologically sustainable. (www. iucn.org)

Centre for International Sustainable Development Law (CISDL) supports understanding, development and implementation of law for sustainable development by leading legal research through scholarship and dialogue, and facilitating legal education through teaching and capacity-building. (www.cisdl.org)

Trust for Sustainable Living and its Living Rainforest Centre exist to further the understanding of sustainable living in the United Kingdom and abroad through high-quality education. (www.livingrainforest.org)

About the 'Voices of Future Generations' Series

To celebrate the 25th Anniversary of the United Nations Convention on the Rights of the Child, the World Future Council (WFC), in cooperation with the Centre for International Sustainable Development Law (CISDL) and other educational charities, the Future Generations Commissioners of several countries, and international leaders from the United Nations Committee on the Rights of the Child, the United Nations Education, Science and Culture Organisation (UNESCO), the International Union for the Conservation of Nature (IUCN), and other international organizations, has launched the new *Voices of Future Generations* Series of Children's Books.

Every year we will feature stories from our selected group of child authors, inspired by the outcomes of the Earth Summit and the recent Rio+20 United Nations Conference on Sustainable Development (UNCSD) and by the Convention on the Rights of the Child (CRC) itself.

Our junior authors, ages 8-18, are concerned about future justice, the global environment, education and children's rights. Accompanied by illustrations, each book profiles creative, interesting and adventurous ideas for creating a just and greener future, in the context of children's interests and lives.

We aim to publish the books internationally in ten languages, raising the voices of future generations and spread their messages for a fair and sustainable tomorrow among their peers and adults, worldwide. We welcome you to join us in support of this inspiring new partnership.

www.worldfuturecouncil.org

about the author

Jona David (9) lives in Cambridge, UK and studies at King's College School. He is a citizen of UK, Canada, Switzerland and Germany, and has authored several Inventor Boy and his Little Brother books.

A Child Delegate to the 2012 UN Conference on Sustainable Development, he is a medallist of the International Schools Debates and Essay Competition on Sustainable Living. He also edits a website on eco-science and technology for kids, and is a Climate Justice Ambassador, leading a pledge to plant over 1000 trees across the world.

Jona enjoys maths and science (especially astro-physics and botany), also chess, reading, polo, swimming, canoeing, aikido and the flute. He loves creating blueprints for eco-inventions, but still needs to figure out how to build them.

He thanks his parents, his Headmaster and his outstanding teachers at King's, and especially his little brother Nico, for their inspiration and help, and also Carol Adlam for her epic drawings.

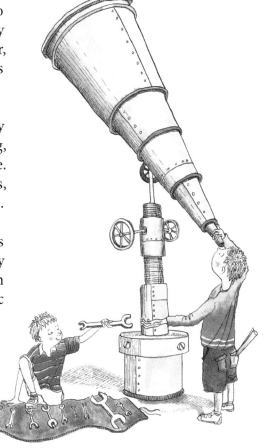

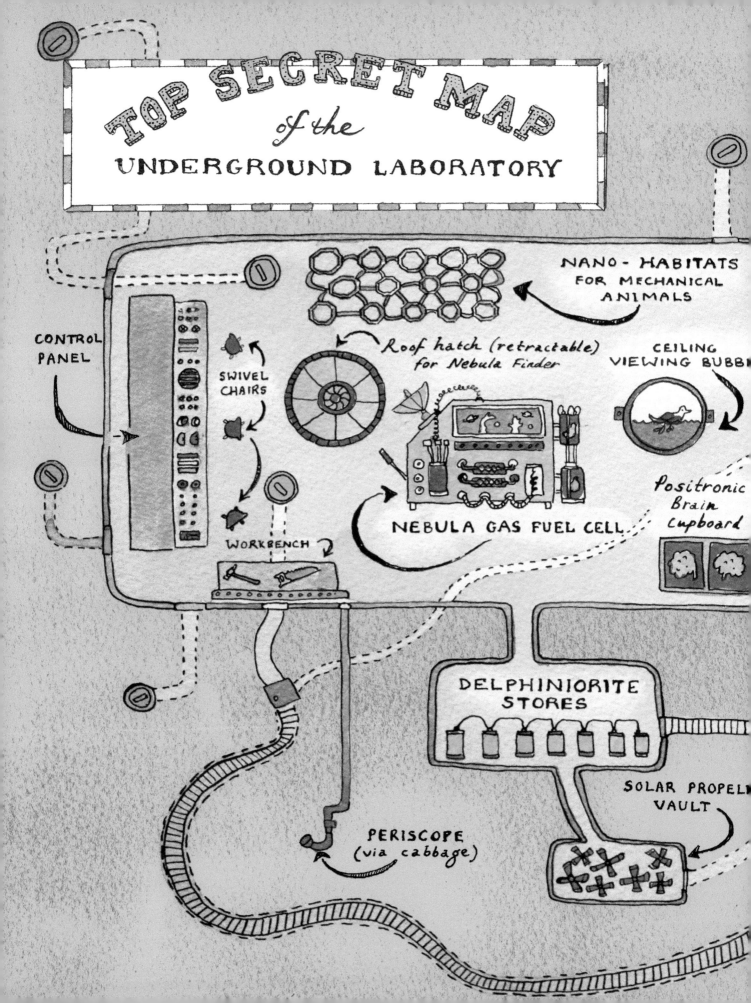

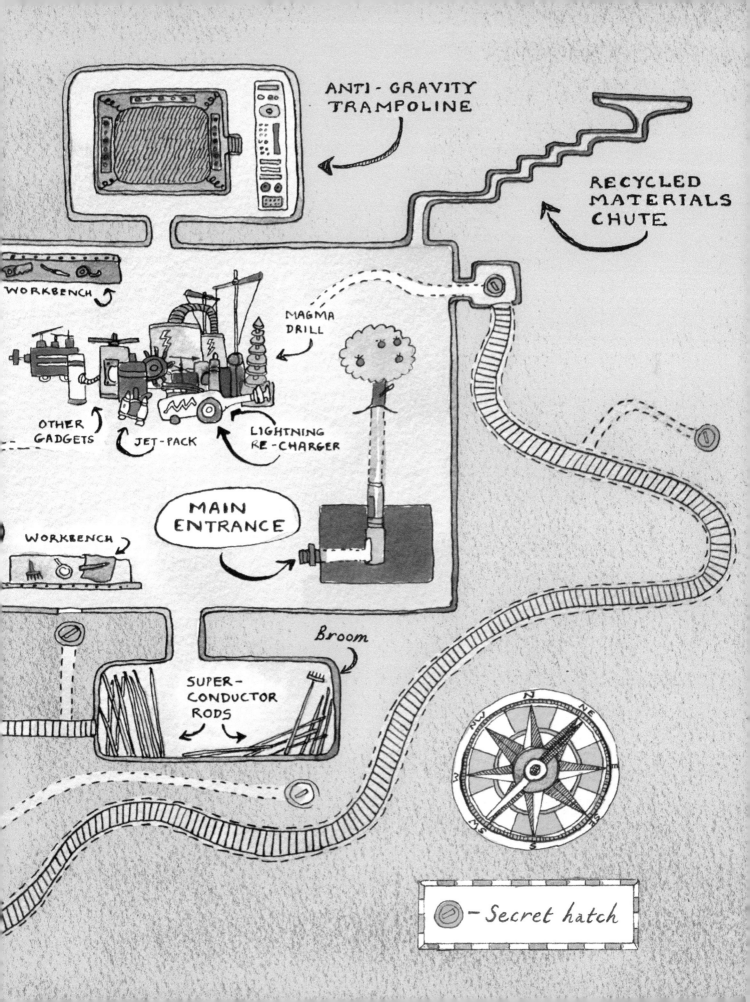

ANTI-GRAVITY TRAMPOLINE

RECYCLED MATERIALS CHUTE

WORKBENCH

MAGMA DRILL

OTHER GADGETS

JET-PACK

LIGHTNING RE-CHARGER

WORKBENCH

MAIN ENTRANCE

Broom

SUPER-CONDUCTOR RODS

- Secret hatch